BIONICLE®

Web
of the Visorak

BIONICLE®

FIND THE POWER,
LIVE THE LEGEND

The legend comes alive in these exciting BIONICLE® books:

BIONICLE™ Chronicles

#1 Tale of the Toa
#2 Beware the Bohrok
#3 Makuta's Revenge
#4 Tales of the Masks

The Official Guide to BIONICLE™

BIONICLE™ Collector's Sticker Book

BIONICLE™ Mask of Light

BIONICLE® Adventures

#1 Mystery of Metru Nui
#2 Trial by Fire
#3 The Darkness Below
#4 Legends of Metru Nui
#5 Voyage of Fear
#6 Maze of Shadows

BIONICLE®

Web
of the Visorak

by Greg Farshtey

SCHOLASTIC INC.
New York Toronto London Auckland Sydney
Mexico City New Delhi Hong Kong Buenos Aires

For Fiona, Toa of Red Pencil,
and always a joy to work with and to know.

No part of this publication may be reproduced in whole or part, stored
in a retrieval system, or transmitted in any form or by any means, electronic, mechanical,
photocopying, recording, or otherwise, without written permission of the publisher.
For information regarding permission, write to Scholastic Inc.,
Attention: Permissions Department, 557 Broadway, New York, NY 10012.

ISBN 0-439-69619-4

© 2005 The LEGO Group. LEGO, the LEGO logo, BIONICLE,
and the BIONICLE logo are registered trademarks of The LEGO Group
and are used here by special permission.
All rights reserved. Published by Scholastic Inc.
SCHOLASTIC and associated logos are trademarks and/or
registered trademarks of Scholastic Inc.

12 11 10 9 8 7 6 5 4 3 2 1   5 6 7 8/0

Printed in the U.S.A.
First printing, February 2005

INTRODUCTION

Turaga Vakama and Toa Nuva Tahu looked down on the former site of their home village. Ta-Koro had been a mighty fortress whose walls had never been breached by a foe. But that was before the terrible night when the Rahkshi came, raining destruction down and leaving the village to sink into the lava.

"Why have you brought me here?" asked Tahu. "Surely there was some other secluded spot in which you could tell me your tale of Metru Nui."

"There are many such spots," Vakama agreed. "But none that will serve as well as this one. You see, Tahu, this was your home on the island, and now it is gone. When Ta-Koro fell, you felt loss, grief, guilt, rage . . . isn't that so?"

"You know it is."

"Then it is the best place for you to try to understand the history I have to share with you," the Turaga of Fire continued. "One thousand years ago, there were six heroes, the Toa Metru, of whom I was one. We lived in a great city called Metru Nui. But Makuta struck at our city, and despite our best efforts, the Matoran were imprisoned and the city . . . the city was damaged worse than we could know."

Vakama shook his head slowly as the painful memories flooded his mind. "We escaped and found a new home, this island we call Mata Nui. But we had to return to save the Matoran and bring them here. There was no other way."

"You sound as if you regret doing it," Tahu said, puzzled. "You were Toa. Protecting the Matoran was your duty. What else could you do but try to rescue them?"

"We could have done it with wisdom!" snapped Vakama. "We could have done it with unity! If we had, perhaps the horror that was the

Hordika would never have happened . . . perhaps the web of the Visorak would never have been spun."

"Hordika . . . Visorak . . . I don't know these names," Tahu replied.

"Be glad you do not," said Vakama. "Be glad they do not haunt your dreams as they have done mine for, lo, these thousand years."

Vakama reached into his pack and removed a black stone. Tahu knew it well. When stories of the past were told in the sand, this stone represented the evil Makuta, enemy of all Toa and Matoran.

"I don't understand," said Tahu. "You and the other Toa Metru defeated Makuta and imprisoned him in an unbreakable shell of solid protodermis. Surely he was not lying in wait for you when you returned to Metru Nui?"

Vakama held up the stone. "No. Tell me, Tahu, have you ever really looked at this Makuta stone? It is no ordinary rock gathered from the beach of Mata Nui. No, it is far more than that. It is . . . a reminder. And before my tales are done, you will know how it came to be."

As darkness fell, Vakama began to speak once more of times long past. Tahu sat silently, taking in his words, and fighting a strange sensation. Had he not known better, he would have sworn that the shadows themselves had gathered to listen to Vakama's tale.

1

In his brief time as Toa, Vakama had come close to being crushed by Morbuzakh vines, devoured by stone rats, and absorbed into Makuta's essence. He knew that he risked death every time he challenged a foe. By now, he had envisioned a hundred different ways he might meet his end.

As it turned out, though, the Toa of Fire was about to die from a cause that would never have made his list in a million years: white-hot flame. Falling to his knees before the onslaught of his enemy, one thought kept going through his mind.

The other Toa will never believe this.

His mission had started out simply enough. The Toa Metru had finally made it to the shores of the silver sea that surrounded the city of Metru Nui.

In the heart of that city, far beneath the Coliseum, were hundreds of pods containing sleeping Matoran. Unless the Toa could rescue them, these Matoran might slumber for all eternity. It was to save their friends that the Toa had made the journey back to the sea.

Unfortunately, they had forgotten one thing. On their first trip across the ocean, the Toa had sailed a Vahki transport with pods lashed to the bottom to keep it afloat. Pods and transport were now on the beaches of the island refuge the Toa had discovered. With no boat, the only other option was for those Toa who flew to carry those who did not across the ocean, far too great a distance to be practical.

That left only one choice, searching until they found some other way to make the journey. Matau had volunteered to look for old chutes that might traverse the bottom of the sea. Onewa and Whenua were going to try to build a craft, if they could find the right raw materials. Nokama and Nuju were convinced that there was some ancient vessel hidden nearby, left behind by whoever had carved the tunnels to the surface. None of these plans sounded very likely to succeed to Vakama, so he had gone off on his own to explore.

He had discovered a number of vaulted chambers left over from when Makuta had used this area as a base. Most had long since been abandoned by whatever Rahi the dark one had left on guard. Unfortunately, there was nothing to be seen that would be of help to the Toa Metru.

He was about to turn back and join Nokama and Nuju when he spotted another vault door. This one was so well camouflaged by its stony exterior that it looked like just another part of the tunnel wall. Reasoning that anything Makuta wanted to keep hidden would have some value, Vakama melted the lock and opened the massive gateway.

The dim glow of a single lightstone illuminated the chamber. The walls were lined with shelves, all of them cluttered with Vahki and Kralhi parts. Other robotic limbs and clockwork mechanisms were scattered around the floor. It looked like one of the Vahki assemblers' villages back in Po-Metru where the mechanical order enforcers had been constructed.

Why would Makuta have all this? Vakama wondered. *The Vahki were a Matoran creation, intended to protect us. Makuta had nothing to do with their creation, unless . . .*

The Toa of Fire frowned. The Matoran had been very careful to design the Vahki so that they would not cause physical harm. It was possible that Makuta had been attempting to redesign the order enforcers to make them more vicious and dangerous for his own purposes.

Metru Nui will not miss you, Makuta, Vakama thought. *I only pray you stay trapped forever.*

Something else caught his eye. He shoved aside some of the Vahki parts to uncover a pair of insectoid legs, the same ones used for Vahki transport locomotion. Searching a little more uncovered more transport parts. He allowed himself a moment to consider the irony that Makuta's experiments might end up helping to save the Matoran, then began gathering the parts in the center of the chamber.

A blast of heat struck him from behind, as intense as a flame geyser from a Ta-Metru fire pit. Vakama turned to see something taking form in front of the doorway. At first, it was simply a red and orange blur surrounded by shimmering waves of heat. Then it coalesced into a figure of flame, blazing between Vakama and the exit.

"Can you speak?" asked the Toa of Fire.

The flame creature did not respond.

"If you serve Makuta, your master will not be returning," Vakama continued. "You can leave this place. Do you understand?"

The creature blazed even brighter. Even Vakama, whose Toa form was resistant to fire, had to stagger back a step from the sheer magnitude of the heat. As if sensing weakness, the creature began to advance.

Vakama rapidly loaded and launched a Kanoka disk. A tongue of flame reached out from his foe's body, encircled the disk, and melted it in midair.

The Toa of Fire hurled a ball of fire, already suspecting it would be ineffective. The creature responded with one of its own, and the two collided, canceling each other out. Vakama struck again, this time melting the stone floor under his opponent's feet. The fire being never moved. Instead, it used its powers to create a thermal updraft that held it aloft.

I could learn some things about my powers from this creature, thought Vakama. *The problem would be living long enough to put them to use.*

The temperature in the chamber, already high from the battle, began to rise even more. The fire being was acting as a furnace, trying to weaken Vakama with intense heat before finishing him off. To the Toa's surprise, it was working. He could see the Vahki and transport parts beginning to soften and melt, and worse, feel his own Toa armor melting as well.

I use fire, but it is fire, he thought. *A nova blast might stop it . . . but it would also destroy these tunnels and the other Toa in them.*

Vakama racked his brain. There had to be a way to defeat this thing! He found himself wishing Nuju were there, both for his knowledge of tactics and his ice power. Maybe the cold could counteract . . .

The Toa of Fire stopped short. Cold was the answer, and perhaps he didn't need Nuju for that. It was something he had never tried before. But there was no time to gauge the risks, not if he wanted to avoid becoming a puddle of proto-dermis on the floor.

He reached out with his elemental powers, mustering all his concentration and forcing himself to ignore his weakness. In the past, he had saved himself and Onewa by absorbing open flames into his body. This was something far more dangerous: actually absorbing all the heat in the room.

Little by little, the temperature in the chamber began to drop. The fire being seemed confused, pushing itself more and more to fight off the sudden cold. Vakama was relentless, calling on more of his power and drawing every last degree of heat into himself. The Toa's body glowed like a star. Through a red haze, he could see ice forming on the walls and floors. Now it was the fire creature's turn to back away, trying to escape the fatal chill.

Vakama pushed himself to his limit, and then beyond. The cold was making his limbs feel like lead. More power than he had ever known threatened to consume him. The fire being stumbled backward and collapsed, frost forming atop its flames. As the Toa of Fire watched, a thick coating of ice covered his foe.

The Toa of Fire knew in that moment he had won, but there was no cause to celebrate. He was almost frozen solid and perilously close to passing out. If he lost consciousness, the power within him would run wild and explode outward, killing himself and who knew how many others.

He forced himself to move, the sheath of ice that covered his body cracking as he did so. He raised his arms, ignoring the fact that it felt like he was trying to lift the city of Metru Nui. Then Vakama unleashed his newfound power, blasting the back wall of the chamber to atoms, along with the miles of tunnel that stretched beyond it.

In the last moment before the darkness closed in, the Toa of Fire realized that he had just faced, and conquered, a dark version of himself.

But I don't think I could do it again.

When the other Toa found him, he was still lying unconscious among the rubble. The fire being was gone. Nokama used cooling water to revive him as the others gathered the pieces of the transport. It would take some effort to repair the parts and put the vehicle back together, but it seemed their best option.

That left them with only one problem. "It won't swim-float," pointed out Matau. "The other transport stayed afloat for maybe a minute before we lashed the pods to the bottom. And we have no Matoran-pods to use this time."

"No, but we might have something that can replace them," said Onewa. "Come with me, and bring your aero-slicers."

An hour later, the two Toa returned, both of them carrying armloads of blackened logs. They didn't have to explain where they had got them. The Toa had only recently witnessed the death of the Karzahni, a plant creature created by Makuta with an appetite for conquest. Onewa had decided to put the trunk and branches to good use.

If the idea of using the Karzahni to help them make it back home bothered any of the Toa, they didn't say anything. Vakama welded the parts of the transport together while Onewa, Matau and Whenua turned the logs into a crude raft. When the transport was done, they lashed the raft to the bottom and pushed it into the water. It wasn't the most seaworthy vessel ever to ride the waves, but it didn't sink either.

As they boarded the new boat, christened *Lhikan II*, none of the Toa noticed a small, green shoot growing from one of the logs. It would be an oversight they would come to regret.

. . .

Matau sat in the cockpit. He was just about to start the transport's insectoid legs moving when he noticed Nuju's disapproving gaze.

"What?"

"I think I should drive," said Nuju.

"You?" laughed the Toa of Air. "A Ko-Metru librarian, steer-piloting a machine like this? Why?"

"Because I remember what happened the last time you drove."

"Yes, we only found a beautiful home-island, Nuju. Nothing very important or special," Matau replied, sarcastically.

The Toa of Ice shook his head. "How is it that you manage to remember only the good things, never the bad?"

Matau grinned. "Practice, brother. Lots and lots of practice."

Onewa crouched at the bow of the vessel, his eyes locked on the silhouette of Metru Nui. He expected the city to be dark, and it was, nor was he surprised that only one sun now shone in the heavens. Makuta had drawn upon great and terrible forces when they fought him in Metru Nui. There was no telling what damage might have been done to the city of legends during that conflict.

Still, something about the look of the city was nagging at him. He might not have spent his life in crystal towers like Nuju, or soaring through chutes like Matau, but he knew Metru Nui. He knew its rhythms, its feel, almost as if it were an old and trusted friend. Even stripped of its population, there were things that could not change about Metru Nui.

And yet they have . . .

"What do you see?" asked Whenua.

"Mist, everywhere, shrouding the city . . . can't you spot it yourself?"

"You know my eyes are not strong in the light," said the Toa of Earth. "Maybe that is why I can't see what you do."

"Or maybe you just don't want to." Then, more gently, Onewa continued, "You really didn't want to leave, did you?"

"Of course not. It's our home. Battered, bruised, but still the only place we have ever known. We could have stayed and rebuilt. We still could."

Onewa said nothing. The same thoughts had occurred to him many times over the past few days. It had been Vakama's visions that told them they must move on to a new land, beyond the Great Barrier, a place where Matoran could live in peace. What if the Toa of Fire was wrong?

He pushed the idea out of his mind. True, he had doubted Vakama from the beginning, but each time he had been proven wrong. It was too late to begin regretting the course of action they had all agreed upon. More than that, it was simply too painful to consider the possibility that they were abandoning Metru Nui for nothing.

His eye was drawn to movement in the city. With all the Matoran trapped in slumber, nothing should have been darting across the rooftops. *Could Makuta already be free? Are we sailing into a trap?*

"Nuju!" he called. "I have need of your vision."

The Toa of Ice moved to stand beside him. Onewa pointed to the southern tip of the city. Nuju focused the telescopic lens of his mask on that point. He stared straight ahead for a long minute, never speaking, until Onewa could no longer contain his impatience.

"What is it? What do you see?"

"Something is preparing to welcome us home," Nuju answered quietly. "We should make certain we do not attend the celebration empty-handed."

Whenua watched, puzzled, as Nuju and Nokama practiced complicated tactical maneuvers on the deck. Using both tools and elemental powers, they engaged in mock battle with the same intensity as if they were challenging a Vahki. Nokama hurled water blasts and Nuju froze them; Nuju tried to trip her up with his crystal spikes, only to be felled himself by her hydro blades.

"Is this really necessary?" asked the Toa of Earth. "What is in Metru Nui that we can't handle?"

"It never hurts to be fully prepared," Nuju answered, narrowly evading a blow from Nokama's tool.

"Nuju saw Rahkshi — lots of them — on the rooftops," Nokama said, parrying strikes from the Toa of Ice. "If they have emerged from the tunnels, it must mean the Vahki are either shut down or else too busy to challenge them. Either way, it means things could be worse there than we thought."

"I wish I could have seen more," Nuju continued. "But the mist makes it difficult, and there was something more . . . something I couldn't make out. It was everywhere, obscuring the buildings and spires of the city. I fear for Metru Nui."

Vakama's reaction to the news had been to urge Matau to increase their speed. The Toa of Air was never one to turn down a chance to make a vehicle go faster, but the choppy seas were beginning to make even him nervous.

"The skies are gray-dark," he said. "Lots of lightning, too. Might not be the best time to cross."

"We keep going," answered Vakama.

And then there is what Nuju spotted," said Onewa. "We should send one or two of us ahead as a scouting party. I would volunteer. Make sure we know what we are walking into."

Vakama shook his head. "We can't afford

the delay. I don't want the Matoran trapped in those sleep pods any longer than they absolutely have to be."

"If we end up Rahi bones on the shore, they will be sleeping a good long time," Matau muttered. "Vahki transports are built for calm seas, not storm-tossed."

A wave washed over the deck of the transport. Vakama and Onewa held onto the railing to keep from being swept overboard. But the sea's argument made no more difference to the Toa of Fire than did Matau's.

"Waiting increases the risk that Rahkshi or something else will break into the Coliseum and harm the Matoran," he said firmly. "So we go on. If we wanted smooth seas and safety, we should never have become Toa."

Matau watched the Toa of Fire walk away, and said to himself, "Or one of us shouldn't have, anyway."

Ga-Matoran in Metru Nui had a special fondness for boat racing. In their off-time, they would often gather at the canals with miniature replicas of Ga-Metru vessels and sail them against each other to see which was the fastest. The truly daring would wait for those times when the channels were opened to the sea and huge tides of liquid protodermis would sweep through the canals. More than one little boat was swept up by the current in those races and smashed to shards against the walls.

Nokama was beginning to get an idea of how those vessels felt. Twin storms had converged on the *Lhikan II*, hurling it this way and that. Tidal waves threatened to swamp or sink the boat. Vakama had ordered Nuju, Whenua, and Onewa below to lessen the chance they would be swept overboard. He remained near the cockpit, keeping watch as Matau struggled to keep the transport on course for Metru Nui. For her part, Nokama was straining her elemental powers to try to calm the raging seas.

"It's no use!" she cried. "The storm is too strong for me to control! We need to turn back!"

"Nowhere to turn back to now!" shouted Matau. "It stretches all the way to the Great Barrier. Forward-sail or backward-sail, the end is the same."

"If we can't outrun it, we will just have to plow through it," said Vakama. "Keep on course."

"I never knew Ta-Matoran were such ever-smart sailors," snapped the Toa of Air. "What do you think I'm trying to do?"

The ocean ended the argument. A massive swell lifted the vessel high into the air. At the apex, a lightning bolt slammed into the bow, shearing off a large chunk of the hull. Then the wave pitched the ship forward, sending it plunging at high speed toward the shoreline of Metru Nui.

"Hang on!" shouted Vakama.

Like one of those miniature Ga-Metru toy boats, the *Lhikan II* slammed into the sea and disintegrated on impact. The tide swept the shattered pieces of the transport and the Karzahni cuttings in every direction, but of the Toa there was no sign.

. . .

A small Rahi reptile skittered across the rubble-strewn shores of Le-Metru. Now and then, small fish would work their way this close to the city's edge and become trapped among the rocks, making them easy prey. The larger animals stayed away from the water, especially in a storm, so it was a safe place to find a meal.

Something stirred in the muck. The reptile paused, eyes wide, waiting to see if it was dinner or some marine predator driven to shore by the violent seas. When Toa Onewa's head popped up out of the mud, the Rahi leapt in fright and raced off.

"Well, that . . . stunk," said the Toa of Stone.

A second figure rose up, covered in mud and seaweed, looking like a creature even an archivist couldn't love. Onewa let out an involuntary cry of surprise and struggled to free his proto pitons from the mud. The figure raised a muck-encrusted arm and scraped the mud from its face, revealing the familiar mask of the Toa of Ice.

"It would appear there was an error in our transport," he said slowly. "*Pilot* error."

Matau's head and shoulders suddenly burst from a pile of rubble between the two Toa. He shot Nuju a look of annoyance. "Hey, I was only order-taking. Vakama was order-giving."

"No need to be critical, Matau."

The three Toa turned to see Nokama emerging from the water. "Regardless of how gracefully," she continued, "we made it."

"Yeah, well . . . whatever," grumbled Matau. His attempt to shrug was foiled by the rock and mud that surrounded him. "Could somebody dig me out of here?"

Whenua approached and used his earth-shock drills to clear away some of the debris. Then he reached down, grabbed Matau's hand, and pulled the Toa of Air loose.

"Thanks," said Matau.

"It's what I do," replied Whenua. "Good to see we are all intact. But where is — ?"

"Are we going to stand around all night?"

yelled Vakama, emerging from the darkened streets of the city. "Or are we going to rescue Matoran?"

The little Rahi reptile ran as fast as its legs could carry it. It had seen many strange things since the great shadow fell on the city, but tall ones who spring from mud were something new and most unwelcome. So panicked was the tiny creature that it never stopped to think just where it was heading until it was too late.

It rounded a pile of shattered masonry at top speed and hit a thin, but strong, web head on. Its own struggles to free itself only entangled it more, until it hung helplessly waiting for its captor.

After a few moments, the weaver of the web appeared. The black spider-creature eyed its catch with disdain. It had hoped for one of the larger Rahi who were running wild through the city. Instead, here was this miniscule, jabbering thing, barely worth wasting a cocoon on.

The reptile was panicked. It knew far too well what this creature was — it had seen the like all over Le-Metru. Bigger Rahi ran in terror from the spiders, but they never made it very far. Most wound up wrapped in webs, not quite dead, not quite alive.

Thinking quickly, the little creature decided that if it explained its trespass, maybe the spider would let it go. It spoke rapidly, relating how it was simply looking for a meal when these larger beings with two faces chased it.

The spider paused. The beings described sounded suspiciously like the ones Roodaka had demanded the hordes watch out for. Perhaps there would be some use for this Rahi besides just the usual. Roodaka might even reward the messenger that brought such news.

The Visorak spider plucked the squirming reptile from the web with its mandibles and began the long journey to the Coliseum.

Roodaka tapped her claws on the arm of her throne, deep in thought.

Strictly speaking, of course, it was not her throne. It belonged to Sidorak, master of the Visorak hordes. But he was away, overseeing another hunt, which was fine with her. Sidorak was a skilled commander, and had his uses, but his company could be tiresome to say the least. She needed time to plan.

Her peace was disrupted by a Visorak called Oohnorak carrying a small Rahi in its jaws. The interruption irritated her, which did not bode well for her visitor. Visorak who annoyed Roodaka rarely lived to see another hunt.

"It is too small to be tribute," she said, eyeing the struggling Rahi, "and too scrawny to be lunch. So I assume this sad, malodorous creature serves some other purpose? Some *extremely important* purpose?"

Oohnorak squeezed his mandibles a little tighter on the Rahi. His catch responded by babbling out the entire story again. Roodaka listened, bored at first, then gradually growing more interested when it became obvious who the little creature had encountered.

"So the Toa have returned, as I knew they would," she said softly. "They conquered Makuta, but they left without their prize, those wretched little Matoran. No one can ignore the spoils of victory, not even heroes. It was only a matter of time."

She gestured to the Rahi. "Set the puny beast free."

The Visorak looked at her. Something about its attitude suggested it was actually considering questioning her order. Then, realizing what a fatal mistake that would be, it opened its jaws and let the reptile scamper away.

"Let it enjoy a few more hours of life," Roodaka said. "This city is ours. Where can it go? As for the Toa . . ."

She rose, the dim light reflecting off her sleek, ebon form. "Find them. Now. And when they are found . . . you know what to do."

Roodaka watched the Visorak depart to carry out her commands, and allowed herself a smile. Fate had delivered right into her claws — the only thing she needed to complete her plans. Now it was just a matter of time.

The Toa Metru walked through the quake-damaged Le-Metru. Their progress was slow. Most of the city's lightstones had gone dark, and those that still worked produced only dim illumination. The streets were strewn with rubble and strange plants had overgrown entire blocks. This, combined with the absence of any Matoran, created the impression of a dead city. Worst of all were the webs, a combination of thick and thin strands with the strength of solid metal that hampered all forward movement.

Whenua was up ahead, using his Mask of Night Vision to try and light the way, accompanied by Matau. Vakama and Nokama stayed close behind, with Onewa and Nuju on their flanks.

"Where were you? I mean, after we crashed," asked Nokama.

"Scouting," the Toa of Fire replied. "I wanted to make sure there was no immediate danger."

"You might have helped your brothers first. They could have been injured. I'm surprised you didn't think of that."

Vakama paused for a moment before

replying. "I did. But if I went looking for them, and there was something lurking nearby, we might have been caught unaware. I made a decision to scout first, and seek later."

Nokama said nothing. They walked on in an uncomfortable silence for a while before she turned back to him. "You don't have to feel bad, you know."

"About what?"

"The wreck. Even if we had turned back earlier, we might still have been swept up in the storm. It wasn't your fault."

Vakama glanced at her, as if surprised she had brought it up. "I don't feel bad. We had to get back to Metru Nui. I wasn't going to let a little rain get in our way."

A little rain? Nokama shook her head. She had seen Vakama angry, frightened, confident, uncertain, and in a whole host of other moods, but this new attitude was beyond her. She wasn't sure whether to be irritated or worried by his recklessness.

As if sensing that she did not approve of his

actions, Vakama stopped and looked her in the eyes. "Listen. Toa Lhikan was captured by the Dark Hunters because I could not help him. He gave me a mission — save the heart of the city, the Matoran — and I failed. He died taking a blast meant for me, because I wasn't good enough to stop Makuta before that."

Vakama's eyes blazed. "I won't fail again. The Matoran will be saved, with the rest of you . . . or without you."

"This is not Le-Metru," Matau repeated for the fifth time. "It is a bad thought-dream."

"I am sorry," said Whenua. "But it is real. And I am sure the rest of the city looks just as bad."

"Nothing could be as bad as this," Matau replied. "So many chutes broken . . . streets buckled . . . green-growth everywhere . . . buildings shattered . . . if this is what happens when we win a fight, I hope we never lose one."

"It could all be repaired," Whenua said quietly. "But Vakama says we have to leave and start fresh on the island."

"The thought of trying to fix all this does not bring happy-cheer," said Matau. "But neither does trying to ride Ussal carts through that swamp in our new home."

"What do you really think of his visions?"

Matau shrugged. "They have been right, so far." He paused, before adding, "Often enough that we might follow one's lead, even if he simply made it up."

Whenua looked at Matau. Had the Toa of Air just suggested that the entire move to the island might be the result of a lie on the part of Vakama? Why? What could Vakama hope to gain by leading them to a strange new land?

The problem with questions, he decided, *is that they are impossible to forget, once they have been asked. If you cannot forget them, then you have to find answers for them, even when you would rather not.*

He was almost grateful for the noise that interrupted his thoughts. It had come from off to the right, site of some of the thicker vegetation that now choked the streets. Something was in there, most likely a Rahi. Whenua silently signaled for Matau to circle to the right and see if he could flush out the creature. Once it was out in the open, the Toa of Earth could use his Mask of Night Vision to blind it until it could be subdued.

Matau had gone perhaps four steps into the tall grass when he found himself tangled in web. Unlike some of the other ones that had been old and brittle, this one was fresh and stubbornly clung to him. He started to hack at it with his slicers before realizing that thrashing about would just draw the attention of the hidden Rahi.

He was half-right. His movements did attract unwanted notice, but not from Rahi. Instead, three Vahki Rorzakh rose out of the tangle of grass and vines. Their eyes flashed scarlet as they spotted Matau, now helplessly tangled in the web.

As one, the Vahki shifted from four-legged to two-legged mode. As one, they raised their stun staffs and aimed them at Matau. Even more shocking, as one — they spoke!

"Surrender, intruder . . . or perish."

Matau braced himself and prepared to move. Vahki stun staffs affected the mind only, so he didn't have to worry about physical damage. The trick would be dodging while stuck in the web.

"Surrender, intruder," the Vahki repeated. Their voices were harsh, mechanical, and riddled with static. That was not half so disturbing as the fact that they even *had* voices. Vahki had always communicated via ultrasonics, never in an understandable language.

Matau heard Whenua's earthshock drills revving. So did the Vahki, two of their number breaking off to investigate. "Whenua, watch out! Vahki!" the Toa of Air shouted.

One of the remaining Vahki unleashed a blast from his stun staff. Matau barely managed to duck his head out of the way. The bolt struck the web and promptly incinerated a large portion of it.

Behind his mask, Matau's eyes widened. Vahki stun blasts couldn't do that! They were specifically designed not to cause property damage or injure Matoran. What was going on here?

Another blast sounded to his left. He heard Whenua grunt and hit the ground. The other Toa would be there any moment, but there was no guarantee they would be in time. The Vahki's bolt had weakened the web, not much, but it would have to be enough.

Matau threw himself forward as if he were going to do a somersault. Some of the web ripped away from his back, as his slicers cut through more. Twin bolts struck him before he could free himself, blasting him back through the web and into a clearing. He was loose, but close to unconsciousness.

Whenua was having his own problems. The Vahki had caught him by surprise, the impact from their stun staffs even more so. Now they were standing over him, demanding he decide between surrender or a sudden halt to his life processes.

He went with a third option. Sending forth his elemental power, Whenua caused two pillars of earth to rise rapidly out of the ground, carrying the Vahki high into the air. Then he sat up and sheared through the pillars with his drills, sending the robotic order enforcers plummeting to the ground. As soon as they recovered from the shock, they would go into flight mode, but that gave Whenua time to head back for the other Toa.

He was halfway down the path when he heard two crashes behind him. Looking back at the sparking, ruined machines, he wondered why they hadn't thought to fly.

The two Vahki lay silent, their robotic bodies mangled by the fall. Then, with painful slowness, their mechanical parts began to twist and bend, reshaping themselves. Limbs that had been twisted beyond repair were now straight and whole again. Shells that had been all but shattered were made solid once more.

Light returned to the eyes of the Vahki. They rose, using their staffs as forelegs and listening intently for the sounds of intruders. Hearing something that seemed out of place, they quietly moved down the path Whenua had followed.

Their programming was crystal clear. Their duty, as it had always been, was to prevent disorder in the city of Metru Nui. Unfortunately, living creatures were a constant source of disturbance to the natural order of things. But although the recent cataclysm had badly damaged the city, it had also opened the Vahki's eyes to a simple truth that changed their mission forever.

After all, there would be no disorder in Metru Nui . . . if there was nothing left alive.

4

A pair of Visorak clung to a web high above the district of Le-Metru. Any other creature would have been unable to see much of anything below, due to the thick vegetation and dense mist. But the keen eyes of the Visorak saw all that went on in the ruined streets of Metru Nui.

The Earth Toa and the Air Toa had joined forces again and were approaching the others. All to the good — the hunt would go faster if they were all together. The Visorak were about to send a signal through the web to summon others of their kind when they spotted more movement in the streets. Vahki. Perhaps a dozen of them were now closing in on the Toa's location.

This was a problem. Roodaka demanded that these Toa be brought to her, not necessarily alive. However, the Vahki would leave nothing, not even remains, to be presented to the queen. In that case, her wrath would be terrible indeed.

One of the Visorak set the web to vibrating, a message that would be picked up by its kind all over the district. All were instructed to monitor the Toa and the Vahki and, if necessary, take action. How shocked the heroes of Metru Nui would be if they discovered the identities of the ones who had saved their lives.

Later on, of course, after they had met the Hordika, the Toa would probably wish they were dead. And who could say, perhaps if she were feeling generous, Roodaka might oblige them.

"Vahki that talk?" asked Nuju, his voice heavy with disbelief. "And fire destructive blasts? I think the strain is getting to you, Matau."

"I saw it too," said Whenua. "They were ready to kill me."

"But they didn't," Vakama cut in. "And we don't have time to worry about Vahki. We have Matoran to save. If they get in our way, we will deal with them then."

"*If* they get in our way?" snapped Matau. "They weren't throwing a happy-surprise Naming Day for us back there!"

"Relax, Matau," said Onewa. "Did either one of you notice anything different about the Vahki? How they looked?"

Matau shook his head immediately. Whenua thought for a long moment, and then said, "Yes, there was something. I hardly noticed at the time, but . . . there were marks on their skull casings. Scorch marks."

Onewa turned to the Toa of Air. "Where is the central taskforce hive for Le-Metru?"

"Near the Moto-Hub. Why?"

"Let's go," said the Toa of Stone. "I think I know what happened here. And if I'm right, Vakama, getting the Matoran out of Metru Nui just became much more difficult."

Matau tried not to look at the Moto-Hub as the Toa drew closer to it. As a Matoran, he had spent almost all his spare time there, watching the assemblers work or testing new vehicles on the track. Now a portion of the dome had caved in and vines and creepers covered the outside walls. The surrounding grounds were littered with rubble and vehicle parts. For the first time, Matau considered that maybe the Matoran were lucky to have slept through all this.

"Best not to think about it," said Nokama, as if she had read his mind. "I am hoping we won't have to go to Ga-Metru at all. I dread seeing what has become of my school and the Great Temple."

Matau said nothing. He had already decided to limit his flying as much as possible. The less he saw of the new Metru Nui, the better.

"Over here!" Onewa called. Matau and Nokama hurried to join the others at the remains of the Vahki Le-Metru subdivision hive. Whenua tore the metal door off its hinges while the others braced for a possible attack.

Nothing sprang out at them. Whenua used his mask to illuminate the interior. It was a tangled mess of wires leading to and from power cradles. When not on patrol, the Vahki rested in these frames and were recharged with energy from the power plant.

"Shine the light over here," Onewa said as he began rummaging through the debris. "My first clue was when you said you could understand what the Vahki were saying."

"That's right," answered Whenua. "Everyone knows Vahki don't speak Matoran."

"Correction. Everyone outside of Po-Metru *thinks* they know that," said Onewa. "Remember, an Onu-Matoran may have designed the Vahki, but Po-Matoran built them."

The Toa of Stone fished a charred Vahki head and arm out of the rubble. "Blown to pieces. I bet that happened to a lot of them. Otherwise, the city would be overrun already."

He tossed the robot head to Whenua. "Vahki always spoke Matoran. They just spoke it at such a high pitch and speed that no one could understand them. When you said they were making sense, I knew something had happened that affected their speech centers, and maybe the rest of them too."

Onewa bent down, grabbed one of the power cradles, and with a mighty heave, tore it loose. He dragged it out of the hive and dropped it at the feet of the Toa. The metal frame was scorched and partially melted.

"There. When Makuta overloaded the power plant, the feedback shot through the hives. Most of the Vahki were destroyed by it. The ones who weren't absorbed the energy surge and were . . . changed."

A half dozen energy bolts sizzled through the air around the Toa Metru. The heroes scattered as the blasts tore holes in the hive. Right on the heels of the attack came the sight of three Nuurakh and three Keerakh closing in on the location.

Vakama raised his disk launcher and Nuju his crystal spikes, ready to defend themselves. Matau slipped between them and forced their weapons down. "No!" he whispered. "I don't want Le-Metru damage-scarred worse than it already has been. Hide in the Moto-Hub. I have an idea."

Running and hiding didn't sit well with any of Matau's comrades. But one of the most important parts of being a Toa was respecting the rights of another when in his metru. This was Matau's home, so it had to be his choice. Silently, the other five heroes vanished through a crack in the Moto-Hub wall.

The Toa of Air triggered the power of his Mask of Illusion, transforming himself into a duplicate of a Vahki Rorzakh. He was careful to make sure that the scorch marks Whenua had spotted were in the right place. Once the shapeshifting was done, he stepped boldly out to face the oncoming order enforcers.

The lead Nuurakh looked him up and down. "Hive and subsection," it said.

Matau thought fast. "Um, there is no time to waste on protocol. The intruders have escaped!"

"Hive and subsection," the Vahki repeated.

"I can tell you to which hive and subsection I will be going next: yours, to report you for incompetence," Matau replied. "They were headed for Ta-Metru. If we hurry, we can run them down."

One of the Keerakh stepped forward. "They were here? You saw them?"

"Yes."

"And you let them escape?"

Too late Matau realized he had walked into a trap. "Well, not really . . . you see, they were already . . ."

The Keerakh turned to the Nuurakh, totally ignoring Matau. "A properly functioning Vahki does not allow a lawbreaker to escape. That unit is therefore not functioning properly. I recommend that its processes be completely shut down until repairs can be made."

The Nuurahkh nodded. All six Vahki raised their staffs, aimed them at the Vahki/Matau, and prepared to execute their new command.

Inside the Moto-Hub, the Toa Metru walked carefully among the debris. Whenua had shut down his mask power so that the bright light would not attract the attention of the Vahki. Onewa stumbled on a piece of pipe and almost fell.

"Rahi bones!" he cursed. "I'm guessing this place was a mess *before* the quake."

"When did Po-Matoran start caring about neatness?" asked Nuju.

"When I started tripping over somebody else's junk," Onewa replied. "What's taking Matau so long?"

"He's probably in command of the squad by now," Whenua chuckled. "And leading them to . . ." The Toa of Earth's voice trailed off.

Nokama turned around to look at him. She could barely see Whenua's outline in the dim light. He was facing the wall, examining something she could not make out. "What is it?" she asked.

"Look for yourself," answered Whenua, shining a narrow beam of light onto the metal wall. Hanging from the ceiling was another web, but this one had an added feature that they had not seen before. A partially torn cocoon nestled in the center of the web.

"What do you think that held?" asked Vakama.

"I don't know. But whatever it was, it got out," said Whenua. "And I would guess it is in here with us."

Matau did his best to ignore the stun staffs pointed his way. It had been his decision to send the Toa Metru into the Moto-Hub, while he stayed here to lure the Vahki away. If it hadn't worked, well, at least he could still buy time for his friends to escape. He wondered if his form would immediately shift from Vahki to Toa if he was unconscious or dead. He hoped so — otherwise, the Vahki might decide to disassemble their "malfunctioning" target right on the spot.

The Vahki prepared to launch their energy bolts. Matau waited, eyes open, refusing to give them the satisfaction of showing any fear.

Something caught his eye in the distance. He couldn't make it out clearly, but it seemed to be spinning through the air at a high altitude. As he watched, it dropped rapidly, headed for the Vahki.

The object whirled in front of the order enforcers, striking each of their staffs in turn. Wherever it hit, acid burned through the tools, shearing them in half.

What was that? wondered Matau, watching the spinning object soar away. *And how can I get my hands on one?*

The Vahki whirled and immediately went into a defensive posture. Their optical receptors scanned the area, searching for whoever dared to interfere with their operations. Matau took advantage of their distraction to slip away into the Moto-Hub.

High above, the hard, cold eyes of the Visorak watched events unfold. The Vahki would move off to search for easier prey, while the Toa huddled in the Moto-Hub, foolishly believing themselves to be safe.

One of the creatures unleashed a second whirling sphere of energy, this time burning through an overhanging beam on the face of the Moto-Hub. It crashed to the ground, bringing a ton of masonry with it, blocking the entrance through which the six heroes of Metru Nui had passed. Once that was done, a new signal was sent through the steel like strands that shrouded the city, a summons not to be disobeyed.

And the end of the Toa came crawling, crawling across a thousand webs, a vast moving shadow that engulfed all in its path. Rahi fled at the sight, streaming out of Le-Metru in a blind panic. Those who could not run burrowed beneath the wreckage of a ruined city and shivered in the darkness, one thought holding their hearts in a grip of fear: The Visorak, the stealers of life, were on the march once more.

Matau heard the crash behind him and assumed the Vahki were venting their anger at his disappearance. He moved rapidly through the corridors of the Moto-Hub, searching for the other Toa. As badly damaged as it was, the building was an old friend to the Toa of Air and he could easily navigate it even in darkness.

The voices of the other Toa drifted down from up above. They had evidently traveled in the direction of the test track. Matau found a ladder and began to climb.

The sound of his armored feet striking the rungs roused a creature who slumbered in the darkness. Red eyes snapped open, focusing immediately on the stranger in its new lair. Its long body uncoiled even as leathern wings unfolded to their full span. It launched itself into the air and began to silently follow Matau.

. . .

Despite the severe damage done to the city, the Le-Metru test track had remained relatively intact. Its original construction had included layers and layers of reinforced solid protodermis, proof against even some of the spectacular crashes Matau had been part of. Vakama doubted that even the Vahki's newfound powers could have pierced the walls.

Whenua had brought the remains of the cocoon with him and was examining it carefully. It was unlike any substance he had seen before, thin and delicate yet incredibly strong. It took effort to even tear one of the strands. He triggered one of his earthshock drills at low speed and reached inside to see how easily he could make a hole in the webbing.

The Toa of Earth suddenly grunted in pain and dropped the damaged cocoon on the ground. Whenua looked down at his hand, mystified.

"What's the matter?" asked Nuju.

"Something in that mass of webbing stung

me," Whenua answered, holding out his hand. "Look."

Nuju extended his telescopic lense. Yes, there was a small wound visible. The Toa of Ice retrieved the cocoon and inspected the interior.

"Barbs," he said. "The inside of the cocoon was lined with them." Nuju reached inside and very gently snapped one of the sharp strands of webbing off. A drop of copper colored fluid was pooled inside the barb.

The Toa of Earth frowned. "What is that? Some new kind of energized protodermis?"

Nuju peered intently at the liquid. "No. The color and consistency are all wrong. I think this is something organic . . . some kind of venom, perhaps."

Venom. The word echoed in Whenua's mind. A memory was struggling to come to light. It had first been awakened by Onewa's use of the word "Visorak" while his mind was enthralled by a strange creature in the tunnels between Metru Nui and the island above. Then when the Toa arrived in the city to find it shrouded by webs, the feeling grew stronger. Somehow, in some way, Whenua knew what all this meant, but the knowledge was just beyond his reach.

"What do you think made this cocoon?" the archivist asked.

"I don't know," said Nuju, already walking toward the others. "I don't know far too many things, like what this venom does, how many cocoons there may be, and what they are being used for. But I think our future might depend on finding out."

Matau was almost at the top of the ladder. The entrance to the test track was not far away. He was anxious to tell the Toa all about the spinning object he had seen that could cut through Vahki tools. Something like that might be a real help when it came time to rescue the Matoran from the Coliseum.

He stopped in mid-climb. Something was at the top of the ladder. It was a dark shape, with two arms and two legs but no defined features.

Grasping the sides of the ladder, it was crawling down headfirst toward Matau.

Quick-climbing, but not very big, thought the Toa. *Maybe I can scare it off, instead of having a hard-fight.*

"Clear the way," Matau said loudly. "I am a Toa-hero on a mission. Very powerful, very angry!"

The dark figure paused. Then it slowly and deliberately raised a fist and slammed the wall. An explosion of sound erupted in the chamber, tearing Matau loose from the ladder and sending him plunging to the floor far below.

The other Toa Metru raced down the corridor. Nuju's theory on the cocoon had been forgotten as soon as the sonic shock struck the building. They rounded a corner to find a dark, nebulous figure waiting for them.

Nuju called on the power of his Mask of Telekinesis and hurled a piece of masonry over the creature's head as a warning. To his surprise, the entity hurled itself into the air and allowed the stone to strike it. The impact triggered another sonic explosion, this one hurling the Toa Metru backward and slamming them against the walls.

"That's what I like about Metru Nui," Onewa muttered. "Always something new."

The Toa of Stone summoned a ring of rock to surround their adversary. It took only split seconds to bind the being in stone. Onewa expected it to rage or scream, but the figure's response was a simple shrug. When its substance struck the rock, the newly made prison shattered into fragments that buried themselves in the floor, walls and ceiling. The Toa barely ducked the stones in time.

"Nice try," said Whenua.

"Not nice enough," replied the Toa of Stone. "It's still standing, isn't it? Still . . ."

Onewa went silent. Whenua knew that usually meant his friend was hatching a plan, usually one that involved insane risk and almost no chance of success. Those were Onewa's favorite kind of plans.

"Stay here," the Toa of Stone said finally. "I will be back soon. Keep this thing busy, but whatever you do, don't strike it."

"And what are you going to be doing while we are inviting our friend to play akilini?" asked Vakama.

"I have an idea," Onewa answered, already running and leaping over the creature. "But it needs Matau to work."

"Oh, I see," said Whenua, watching him go. "I was worried there for a moment, but you have an idea that needs Matau to work. That changes everything."

"You're not worried now?" asked Nokama.

"No. Now I'm terrified."

Onewa ran at top speed down the corridor. When he reached the ladder that led below, he dropped to his knees to peer down into the darkness. He suddenly wished he had thought to ask Whenua to swap masks.

"Matau!" he yelled.

"Onewa?" the Toa of Air said weakly. "Where are the others?"

"Fighting up above, and we need you," the Toa of Stone answered. "Are you hurt?"

"Hang-clinging to what's left of the ladder," came the reply. "Sore, but alive."

"Can you fly?"

"Straight down, maybe."

Onewa dug the end of his proto piton into the floor and lowered himself down the hole. He had a general idea of where Matau was now. Extending his piton as far as he could, he stretched the other down toward his fellow Toa. "Grab on!"

An instant later, he felt a tug on the piton. Bracing himself, he told Matau to let go of the ladder. The next moment, Onewa was suddenly supporting the weight of a Toa as Matau swung free in the darkness. Slowly, painfully, Onewa hauled himself and Matau back to the floor above.

"Come on, brother," he said. "We will talk on the way."

By the time they made it back to the other Toa, Matau understood the plan. It had come to Onewa when he recalled Vakama's confrontation with the fire creature, but this idea was even more dangerous than that encounter had been. One mistake and any or all of the Toa would be dead.

The Toa Metru had not fared well in their absence. The creature had apparently grown tired of waiting for an attack and had begun hurling portions of its substance at its enemies. When they struck, it was like standing in the middle of a thunder cloud during a storm. The barrage of sound kept the Toa off-balance and on the defensive.

Onewa and Matau took up positions behind the creature. "Nuju, I need airtight walls on both ends of the corridor. Now!"

If any of the Toa felt like arguing, they chose to wait until the fight was over. Mustering their elemental powers, Onewa and Nuju crafted stone and ice walls behind both their group and their enemy. When they were done, the Toa Metru were sealed into a small portion of the hallway with the nebulous figure.

"Matau?" said Onewa.

"I know, I know. Don't hurry-rush me."

The Toa of Air closed his eyes and concentrated. Vakama had been able to draw heat and fire into himself, so that meant Matau should be able to do the same with air. But he could already tell it was going to be harder than he had imagined, especially with his head still ringing from the explosion.

By now, both Nuju and Vakama had figured out what Onewa had in mind. "Hold your breath," Vakama said to the other Toa. "And whatever you do, don't open your mouths."

Whenua had a response in mind, but a sharp look from Nokama convinced him to keep it to himself. He took a deep breath and kept a wary eye on the dark figure, who was becoming agitated. If it unleashed another sonic boom in this confined a space, they would be scraping the Toa off the walls.

Matau summoned more and more of his power. He had long ago passed his limit, but his task was not yet done. If even a single molecule of air remained in the room, Onewa's plan would fail.

When his instincts told him the space was at last airless, he opened his eyes and nodded to Onewa. The Toa of Stone gestured to Nuju, who hurled a stream of solid ice at the dark being. The Toa braced themselves for another explosion of sound.

Ice struck the gleaming surface of the strange being. But this time, there was no sonic attack in response. Instead, the foe shattered like dark crystal and melted away, leaving no trace behind.

Matau didn't wait for Onewa's signal. He unleashed a hurricane wind so powerful that it blew down one of the stone and ice walls. Then he collapsed to his knees, exhausted.

"What just happened?" asked Nokama.

"Sound," said Onewa. "The creature was made of sound. Strike it and you set off a sonic explosion."

"So Matau created a vacuum," Nuju continued. "If there is no air, there is no sound. We could strike him without being struck in return."

"Amazing," said the Toa of Water. "Is there any end to the new dangers we will find here?"

"A better question is, did this thing come from the cocoon we found?" asked Whenua.

"I don't think so. But I would prefer not to

meet the original contents in a confined space," Nuju replied. "Let's get out of this place."

"Hard-ground entrance is blocked," said Matau. "We will have to use the test track emergency hatch. It's a short high-climb."

The Toa Metru headed for the test track. None of them looked back, preferring for the moment not to know if something was gaining on them.

The Le-Metru test track was designed to determine the performance capability of new vehicles. Designers from different metru would bring their plans to Le-Matoran builders, who would decide what was worth testing and what was not. Then a crude prototype would be built and run on the test track by volunteer drivers like Matau. If the vehicle survived the high speeds, steep ascents, and rapid descents, it might be considered for mass production in the Moto-Hub.

Now, the test track was dark and deserted. As the Toa climbed the ladder that led up through the archway to the emergency hatch, no one spoke.

They were all aware of the good memories that Matau had of this place. He had spent most of his spare time here, and had even been on the track when Toa Lhikan gave him his Toa stone.

The Toa of Air wrenched open the emergency hatch, intended for quick escapes by drivers should their vehicles burst into flame. It was wide enough for two Toa to climb through at a time and he and Nuju were first to exit. They stood on top of the archway, looking up at the sky. Through the perpetual mist, thousands of glittering points of light could be seen.

"Look, brother," Matau said, smiling. "Even in this dark-time, the stars keep shining. I don't think I have ever seen so many, even from Po-Metru. Isn't it beautiful?"

"Get back inside!" Nuju snapped, practically shoving Matau back through the hatch.

"What —?"

"Those aren't thousands of stars looking down upon us, brother," said the Toa of Ice, leaping in after him. "Those are eyes!"

"Gukko birds?" asked Matau, hopefully.

"No," replied Whenua. He was focusing the power of his mask on the wall of the archway, seeing through the metal to the crowd of strange creatures up above.

"Stone rats? Ussal crabs? Really big pro-todites?"

"No, no, and what are you thinking?"

"Then what are they?" demanded Vakama. "Why are they up there, watching this place?"

Whenua turned to the Toa of Fire, but then looked away, as if he could not meet his friend's eyes. "Vakama . . . they are Visorak. They are sitting on the webs they created, waiting, knowing we have to come out sometime."

"Visorak?" Vakama repeated. "Wait, Onewa used that term on our journey back to the city, when his mind was controlled by that strange parasite. If you knew the name, why didn't you say so then?"

"I . . . I didn't make the connection," Whenua said quietly. "It's an obscure reference. I saw a portion of a carving once, long ago, that contained the name. It took actually seeing them and their webs to make me remember."

"You're an archivist!" Vakama exploded. "You are supposed to be able to identify the Rahi we run up against! Otherwise, what good are you?"

The others stared at the Toa of Fire, shocked at the outburst. Whenua, stunned and hurt, said nothing. It was Onewa who jumped to his friend's defense. "If we had turned back when the storm started, or sent a scouting party, like I suggested, we wouldn't be in this mess. But you were in such a hurry to get back here so we could leave again that —"

"I am in a hurry to save the Matoran, as you should be," Vakama shot back. "I made a promise to Toa Lhikan, and I intend to keep it."

"Did you make that promise when you let him get captured, or when he died saving your mask?" the Toa of Stone said, turning away. "I am starting to think it is not very healthy to be your friend."

"Far healthier than being my enemy," Vakama answered, a nimbus of flames surrounding his hands. "If you have a problem with me or my leadership, carver, let's hear it."

Onewa spun on his heel, took three long strides forward, and thrust his mask right up to Vakama's. "I have a problem with you, your leadership, your attitude, and your akilini-headed idea that only you have to live up to the legacy of Lhikan. We all do! We all have friends lying in Makuta-sleep under the Coliseum, and we all want to save them! We all know the price of failure! So get down off your Toa statue before I knock you down!"

Nokama stepped in between them, only to have Onewa take a step back and unlimber his proto pitons. "I will fight alongside anyone — Toa, Rahi, Vahki, even the Dark Hunters themselves — to save the Matoran," said the Toa of Stone. "But Makuta take me if I will be a sidekick to a fire-spitter who couldn't find his way out of a forge!"

Matau's aero-slicer flew through the air and plunged into the ground between Vakama and Onewa. "Stop the loud-shouting! Now! The enemy is out there, not in here. And we cannot win a Toa-victory if we are traveling in six different chutes — someone has to lead."

Nuju glanced at his fellow Toa. This was very bad. How could they save the Matoran, let alone build a new life on Mata Nui, if they persisted in behaving like squabbling ice bats? He made a mental note that, if they survived to see the island again, he would impress upon his Matoran the virtue of self-reliance. *Other beings are just . . . annoying,* he decided. *Never before has so much been spoken and so little of worth said. It makes one question the point of having a language at all.*

"All right," said Onewa, slowly lowering his tools. "This is a bad time for an election. We have a mission to perform, so let's just do it. If you're going to lead, Vakama, then lead, but do it without treating us like we're your little fire drones. If you can't do that, get out of the way."

"And you, Onewa — if you are going to follow, then do it without constant argument," Vakama replied. "Otherwise, stay here. We will come back for you."

"You two are forgetting that we may all be staying here, for a very long time," said Nuju.

"No. No, we won't," Nokama replied, already heading down the corridor. The other Toa followed. "You have all forgotten that there is another way out of this building. If we cannot go up, we will go —"

"Down," Whenua finished for her, "and through the Archives."

"Then let's go," said Vakama. "And I want to hear more about these Visorak on the way."

There was little for Whenua to share. The carving he had seen had been indescribably ancient and far from intact. It described a "poisonous scourge" that ravaged entire domains, imprisoning living beings in its webs. The lucky ones stayed wrapped in the cocoons forever. Those less fortunate emerged from the webs mutated into monsters beyond all imagining.

"Why have we never heard of these things before? If they were in Metru Nui, surely the Vahki would have caught one or two."

"That's just it," said Whenua. He peeled back a section of flooring, opening a shaft for the Toa to climb down. "They shouldn't be here. Remember, before the earthquake, Turaga Dume ordered all the gateways to other lands sealed off. At least, we thought it was Dume ... we could not know Makuta had replaced him."

"He sent Toa to close the passages," Vakama said grimly. "None ever returned."

"They must not have closed them all," said the Toa of Earth. "Visorak do not come from our region. If they are here now, they had to have migrated from elsewhere."

Nuju, lost in thought, had to be reminded by Nokama to start climbing. Their destination was the lower level vehicle assembly plant, from which the Archives could be accessed via floor hatches. But the Toa of Ice could not stop thinking about the image of a horde of dangerous creatures sweeping toward Metru Nui, overrunning everything in their path, or . . .

"Driving them to Metru Nui," he whispered.

"What?"

Nuju stopped climbing. "It all makes sense now. All of those Rahi we encountered on our way back to the city, the ones who were fleeing in terror from the city. They were running away from the Visorak."

"Isn't that a little hard to think-believe?" asked Matau. "So many creatures, big and small, afraid of these . . . well, whatever they are."

Vakama was having no trouble believing it to be true. "Whenua, how many of the Rahi in the Archives are native to Metru Nui?"

There was a long silence as the archivist did some mental calculations. Then he said, "Hardly any. Do you mean to say — ?"

"He does," Nokama said quietly. "All of the Rahi who have attacked our city over time . . . the ones we built Vahki to defend ourselves against . . . they were all fleeing something worse than themselves. They ran from the Visorak until they could run no farther, and wound up here."

"We won't run," said Vakama, an intensity in his voice that was almost frightening. "If the Visorak stand between us and the Matoran, it will be too bad for them."

Nuju glanced upward. Something was blocking the top of the shaft. Then that same something was power diving toward the Toa, screaming as it flew. The sound of its cry tore through the ladder just above Nuju. Freed from the wall, the segment of ladder bent from the Toa's weight, leaving Nuju hanging over empty space.

His attacker had already flown past, heading for the others. A sweep of its long tail knocked Matau and Onewa off the ladder. Vakama, Whenua, and Nokama flattened themselves against the wall to keep from being torn loose themselves.

The Rahi slowed as it reached the bottom, then turned and started another pass. Vakama hurled a fireball as much for the light as to ward off the creature. The bright flare revealed a beast far too familiar to the Toa Metru.

Matau, hovering in the air and hanging onto Onewa, was closest. "It's a Lohrak!" The winged serpents had almost overwhelmed the Toa the last time the heroes were in Metru Nui. It had taken a combination of their Toa powers to seal up the colony.

A second look revealed that this was no ordinary Lohrak. The creatures were nasty, but not particularly large. This one was 10 feet from serpentine head to tip of tail, with a wingspan easily twice that. Only the narrow confines of the shaft were keeping it from flying rings around the Toa Metru.

The Lohrak screamed again, this time shattering the ladder below Vakama into dust. That, too, was new — Lohrak had always been more than happy just to squeeze the life out of prey. Sonic powers were not part of their natural tools.

Nuju had already guessed there was a connection between the sound creature that had assailed them above and the Lohrak's new and more dangerous abilities. Before he could share his conclusion, he lost his grip on the ladder and plunged toward the ground below.

Twisting in midair, Nuju fired a blast of ice from his crystal spikes. The ice block cut off the Lohrak from the Toa, also forming a safe, if not comfortable landing for Nuju. The Toa of Ice landed hard and lay there stunned. Beneath him, the ice began to crack.

"Matau! Grab Nuju!" Vakama shouted.

"I can't lift-carry two Toa!" Matau replied. "We'll all hard-fall!"

"Then drop me!" said Onewa. "I'll be all right."

Nokama hesitated for only a few seconds before saying, "Do what he says. And Matau — I would guess that Lohrak has a hard time making friends. What do you think?"

The indistinct shape of the Lohrak drew closer and closer to the layer of ice. Matau wished for help from the Great Spirit. Then he dropped the Toa of Stone and flew as fast as possible toward where Nuju lay dazed.

Everything happened at once. Onewa hurled his proto piton, digging it into the wall and bringing his fall to a halt. Matau grabbed Nuju and strained to get altitude. The Lohrak screamed, smashing the ice block to pieces. A hail of jagged ice crystals temporarily blinded the creature, hindering its pursuit of Matau.

The Toa of Air put the delay to good use, using his Mask of Illusion to take on the appearance of the Lohrak. If Nokama was right, this thing had seen precious few others like it.

The Lohrak paused in mid-flight. Above it was what looked like another of its kind, with a squirming Toa clutched in its claws. But something was not quite right . . . the scent, the way the wings moved, conveyed a sense of something "other."

Whenua peered at the creature, now close enough to him to touch. "Vakama, look," he whispered. "Those little wounds on its side . . . they're in the same positions as the barbs inside the cocoon. I think this thing came out of there."

"But that cocoon was nowhere near this size."

"Then the Lohrak grew," said Whenua. "And it grew quickly."

"Can we measure it later?" snapped Onewa. "Less archiving, more action, Whenua!"

"Oh, go chew on a rock," the Toa of Earth muttered as he revved up his drills. "Vakama, I have an idea. Maybe if we —"

But the Toa of Fire wasn't listening. He had already jumped from the ladder to grab the Lohrak's tail. The Rahi screamed in protest, sending a devastating shock wave up the shaft. The sheer sonic force blew the Lohrak/Matau and Nuju back up through the hole.

When that did not produce the desired effect — Vakama was still hanging on — the Lohrak took a more direct approach. Whipping its tail back and forth, it slammed Vakama into the sides of the shaft.

Nokama reached out with the power of the Mask of Translation. She did her best to copy the Lohrak's cry, asking what it wanted and why it was trying to hurt them. The creature's answer was a cry of its own that blew a hole through the shaft and the exterior wall on the other side, sending Nokama hurtling out of the building.

"Guess it doesn't want to chat," said Onewa. "But I think it just made us an exit."

"We can't leave without the others," replied Whenua.

"Who says we're going to? Catch Vakama."

"What? He's not falling."

Onewa concentrated. Pincers of stone grew from the sides of the shaft and grabbed the Lohrak's tail, squeezing it hard. It swung its tail about violently, smashing Vakama into the wall. Stunned, the Toa of Fire let go and fell, right into the waiting grasp of Whenua.

"Looked like he was falling to me," said Onewa. "Let's go. We can grab Nokama and come back for the other two."

Onewa, Whenua, and Vakama made it to the gap in the wall just as the Lohrak broke free of the pincers. Before them they could see the darkened city, mist hanging over it, Visorak webs everywhere, and six flying Vahki carrying Nokama. The squad was headed right back to where she had come from, on a straight line for the other Toa.

"Or maybe we can't go that way," said the Toa of Stone.

7

The three Toa scrambled out of the way as the Vahki soared through the opening. The last one carried the barely conscious Nokama. Whenua tap-ped the Vahki on the shoulder with his earthshock drill. When it turned, Vakama grabbed it from behind as Onewa snatched Nokama from its grasp.

The Toa of Stone knew the shaft was going to be no place for Nokama. He swung out through the hole and dug his proto piton into the wall. Now the problem was, which way to go? Up meant running into Visorak, down meant Vahki, Rahi, and Mata Nui knew what else. *Maybe it is not so much a question of where I go, as how fast I get there*, he decided.

Down seemed the better option. Vahki and Rahi he knew . . . Visorak were something un-known. He was more than willing to postpone the pleasure of meeting them until all six Toa were together and ready for a fight.

Throwing Nokama over his shoulder, he began the long climb down the outside of the Moto-Hub. His attention had to be totally focused on the descent. One wrong move would doom them both. Concentrating, he never saw the three Visorak that slipped from their web and began to climb down after him . . .

Matau and Nuju peered over the lip of the hole and were shocked by what they saw. In the few moments they had lain there stunned, a full-scale battle had erupted between the Toa Metru, the Vahki, and the Lohrak. So far, the Lohrak seemed to be winning easily.

The Toa of Air had yet to change back to his normal form. Nuju glanced over and found it disturbing to be side by side with a 10 foot long serpent. "Change back," he said.

"Why?" answered Matau. "Maybe I like being a giant snake. No one would dare to give me grief-trouble now!"

Nuju slowly and deliberately aimed his crystal spike right at Matau's serpent head. "I would, and it wasn't a request. Change back."

"No."

The Toa of Ice shrugged. But instead of launching a blast of ice at Matau, he simply created a thin sheet so clear that it served as a mirror. Then he directed the Toa of Air to look at the reflection of his new face.

One glance and Matau said, "Think I will quick-change back to handsome me."

As the Toa of Air mentally switched off the power of the Mask of Illusion, Nuju rose to his feet. "Good idea. We have to help Vakama and Whenua, and there's no point in giving the Vahki two Lohrak to worry about."

"You have a thought-plan?"

"Don't I always? You are the transport expert — tell me, why do Le-Metru airships only fly so high?"

Matau thought for a moment before replying, "Safety. Fly too high-sky, and then you go straight down, because . . ." He grinned. "Because ice forms."

Nuju nodded and sent waves of frost out of his Toa tools toward the Lohrak. Its wings were soon covered with a thick coating of ice. Despite the creature's great strength, it could not compensate for the added weight and keep them beating. Nor could it use its sonic scream to clear them without destroying its own wings. Sensing the trouble was confined to the shaft, the Lohrak used its powers to blow a bigger hole in the wall and forced itself out into space. Vakama saw it turn in midair and head for Ta-Metru, no doubt seeking a source of heat to melt the ice.

If Nuju was hoping the Vahki would pursue, he was disappointed. Apparently, four Toa Metru close by were worth more than a Lohrak on the wing. "I'd hoped we could avoid a fight," said the Toa of Ice.

"We can," answered Matau. Without another word, he summoned a cyclone in the shaft. The winds swept up Vakama, Whenua, and the

Vahki, lifting them higher and higher toward the opening at the top. Matau crouched down, eyes fixed on the rapidly rotating shapes in the whirlwind. At just the right moment, his hands darted into the windstorm and snatched the wrists of Whenua and Vakama.

Seeing what he was doing, Nuju raced over to get a grip on the two Toa as well. Once certain they were both secure, Matau shut down the cyclone. Startled by the abrupt halt, the Vahki plunged down into the darkness. A few moments later, a resounding crash signaled that the machines had landed.

"That's what's missing from Metru Nui these days," said Matau, hauling Whenua and Vakama up out of the shaft. "Not enough crash-bang."

The three white Visorak spiders watched as Onewa and Nokama vanished underground. This breed of Visorak, known as Suukorak, generally preferred high altitudes where the air was crisp and cold. Roporak were far better suited for a subterranean hunt, but they were gathered on the other side of the Moto-Hub. The Suukorak would just have to proceed, or else report to Roodaka that they had allowed Toa to escape. She would no doubt order them bound up in their own webbing and hung out as bait for flying Rahi.

Shuddering a little at the thought, the Visorak marched in single file after their prey.

Onewa laid Nokama down gently, then tried to get his bearings. They were in the Archives, that much he knew, but carvers rarely bothered to visit this place. He had no clue which direction to travel in or what might be lurking nearby. Whenua would know, but the Toa of Earth was back in the shaft. Everything in Onewa told him that he should go back now and help the others, but he knew that wasn't what they would want. They were counting on him to stay free, and Nokama with him. If anything happened, they might be the only Toa left to carry out the mission.

He waited impatiently for the others to arrive. Nokama stirred. Onewa went to help her to her feet. "Easy. You took the brunt of quite a blast."

"I'm all right. Where are the others?"

Onewa heard the hatch open up above. "That must be them now. I guess they finished off that overgrown rock worm."

The Toa of Stone turned to greet his friends. Instead, he found himself face to face with a Suukorak. A spinning wheel of energy erupted from the creature's back and struck Onewa. Instantly, a field of electrical force surrounded the Toa. It did no damage, but moved with him wherever he went. Worse, the more he tried to break away from it, the faster it began to shrink around him.

Onewa could see the creatures' true plan taking shape through the jagged bolts of lightning. Rather than challenge two Toa, they locked one up inside a prison of electricity so they could focus on the other. As he watched, they spat streams of webbing at Nokama, which she barely blocked with her hydro blades.

Inevitably, despite her skill, some got through. The webbing wrapped around her ankles, toppling her to the ground. The Suukorak moved in.

Then they suddenly stopped dead. An

instant later, Onewa heard voices — it was the other Toa! He glanced up toward the hatchway for only an instant. When he brought his eyes back to Nokama, all three of the spiders were gone as if they had never been there.

The electrical field faded as Vakama and the others entered. Nokama was already struggling to rip the webbing off herself. In answer to the Toa's questions, Onewa said he was pretty certain they had just met Visorak in person.

"They ran off when they heard you coming," said the Toa of Stone. "Nasty, but not very brave, I guess."

"No," said Whenua. "Don't think that. First thing you learn as an archivist is you can't judge Rahi behavior by what we do. That's a good way to wind up a deceased archivist."

Nuju could see Onewa was readying a wisecrack. He spoke quickly and cut the Toa of Stone off. "Then what do you think happened, Whenua?"

"I think they heard us coming and withdrew rather than risk a fight they might lose," said

Whenua. "Why take the chance? We're not going anywhere. They have all the time they need."

"You talk like they are making plans," Onewa replied. "They're just Rahi."

"Rahi who have taken over the city," the Toa of Earth said quietly. "Rahi who are powerful enough to frighten beasts five times their size. Three of them almost defeated two Toa Metru, Onewa, and there are hundreds of them out there . . . maybe thousands."

"All the more reason to keep moving," said Vakama. "We'll work our way through the Archives until we are close to the Coliseum. Then we can get our job done."

"What if these Visorak are in the Coliseum too?" asked Matau.

"I doubt it," Vakama answered. "My guess is that the Vahki are still guarding the place. We will deal with them and get the Matoran out before the Visorak know what we are doing."

The team headed into the Archives, with only Matau lagging a bit behind. *I hope you are right, Toa-brother*, he thought. *But somehow I know you're wrong.*

8

Nokama heard the noise first. It was faint, but unmistakeable — something nearby was in pain.

"We need to go right up ahead," she said.

"The path to the Coliseum is straight, then left," corrected Whenua. "We aren't far."

"I heard something. I think there has been trouble."

"That would be a sudden-shock," grumbled Matau. "No trouble on this ground-walk so far, right?"

Nokama turned to the others. "Go on ahead, if you wish. I will catch up. I have to check on this."

"It is too dangerous to be alone down here just now," Nuju replied. "So we will all go."

Vakama started to protest. Nuju silenced him with a glare. "It is possible what you heard,

Nokama, may be a Visorak trap," the Toa of Ice continued. "In which case, it makes sense for all of us to investigate."

Nokama led the way, with Whenua close behind. "What's down here?" she asked the archivist. "I mean, what was down here before . . . ?"

"Isolation ward. Rahi that were constantly attacking archivists and each other were sent down here. If it seemed their behavior wouldn't change, they were moved down to the deeper sublevels where security was better."

"So anything on this level is dangerous?"

Whenua chuckled. "No more dangerous than laying down in front of a Kikanalo stampede. There's a reason that only the real akilini-heads on the staff were assigned here — no point in risking good workers being hurt."

The cry came again, this time loud enough for all of the Toa to hear. Whenua put a hand on Nokama's shoulder and slipped past her. "Better let me go first," he said. "You have to know how to approach a wounded Rahi and gain its trust. Otherwise —"

A huge paw slashed out of the darkness, hurling Whenua backwards against the wall. He slammed into the stone and toppled forward, barely getting his hands out in time to catch himself.

"Otherwise you get knocked on your mask," said Onewa.

Nokama took a step into the darkness. A harsh growl greeted her from within. "Sister, don't!" said Matau.

The Toa of Water ignored him. She kept her eyes forward, trying to pierce the shadows. She could just barely make out a large shape huddled on the stone floor. "Shhhh, it's all right," she said softly. "No one is here to hurt you. Let me help."

"Be ready," Onewa whispered to Nuju. "If that thing attacks —"

"Give Nokama her chance. I don't claim to understand her instincts in these situations, but she seems to have a connection to the natural world that we lack."

"And she can keep it," said the Toa of Stone.

Nokama took another careful step. The Rahi lashed out weakly, its paw never even reaching her. "It's all right. You're not alone anymore." Without turning her head away from the Rahi, she said, "Whenua, shine your light here."

The Toa of Earth did as she asked. The beam from his Mask of Night Vision revealed a young ash bear roughly the size of a Toa. Even an untrained eye could see that she was badly hurt.

"Trampled," Whenua said sadly. "She must have been caught in a rush to get out of here after the quake. I don't think she will last very long, Nokama."

The Toa of Water knelt beside the Rahi. The ash bear was too exhausted and in too much pain to fight. Nokama summoned a cooling mist to comfort the beast. "Is there anything we can do?" she asked Whenua. "We can't just leave her here to die."

"We may not have a choice," said Onewa. "Don't forget there are Visorak down here, and maybe Vahki, and who knows what else. We can't take the time to play healer for a Rahi."

"The Matoran need us," added Vakama. "We have to go."

"The Matoran have been asleep for weeks, unaware of what is going on around them," Nokama shot back. "This creature is alone and afraid . . . and I will not see any being die with fear in its heart."

Nuju looked over the Rahi. The ash bear's injuries were too severe to move her. Of them all, only Whenua really knew anything about taking care of Rahi, and he was ready to give up. That was all the evidence Nuju needed that the animal had no future.

"Let's go, sister," said Onewa. "It's just a Rahi."

"Yes. Yes, it is," said Nokama. "And to Makuta, our friends were all 'just Matoran.' Beings that were not as smart or powerful as he, so not worth caring about. We are supposed to be better than that. Go on, if you want to, I am staying with her."

"Toa-power," said Matau. All eyes turned to him. He looked startled at first, as if not realizing he had spoken aloud. "Toa-power . . . maybe that can help somehow. Look what the energies did for us. Maybe if we work together —"

"It's never been done," answered Whenua.

"Ever been tried?" asked Matau.

"Well . . . no."

"Then that's why it's never been done," said the Toa of Air. "If we stop loud-shouting and at least try it . . . and it doesn't work . . . I am sure Nokama will be willing to ground-walk with us again. Right?"

Nokama shrugged. "All right. If it will get the rest of you to help, I promise — if it fails, we make her as comfortable as we can and then we go."

The other Toa nodded in response.

"Good-fine! We are agreed," said Matau. "So . . . what do we do?"

Nokama knelt by the head of the ash bear, her hands cupped above its face. Matau knelt by the Rahi's feet. Two Toa were on each side, Toa tools extended and crossing each other.

"We have to all act as one," said Nokama. "Concentrate. We have grown so used to using our powers to fight; maybe we have ignored their ability to heal."

One by one, the Toa summoned their unique elemental energies. The outflow of power had to be tightly controlled — it would not do to burn, freeze, or encase the Rahi in stone. As Nokama formed a sphere of water in midair, the other five Toa Metru focused miniscule amounts of their raw energy into it. When it was fully charged, Nokama released the sphere and let the liquid wash over the ash bear.

The Toa watched, questions racing through their minds. Would this treatment cure the Rahi, or kill her? What effect would surrendering even a small amount of their Toa power have on them? None of them knew whether Toa energy reconstituted itself over time, or whether any amount expended was gone for good.

The ash bear twitched and tried to raise her head. It took her a few tries, but once she had fully revived, she let out a roar and rolled onto her feet. The Toa Metru instinctively took a step back, but the Rahi made no move to attack.

She simply regarded each of them in turn, meeting their eyes but not making a sound. Then she gently pushed past Whenua and Nokama and lumbered into the darkness.

"That . . . was amazing," said Nokama.

"Now she has to find a place of safety," said Whenua. "I am not so sure there are any on Metru Nui these days."

"She will be fine," assured Matau. "One day, she will be quick-bounding out of the trees on the island up above, scaring the masks off of Matoran. Wait and see."

"There won't be any Matoran there if we don't get moving," said Vakama. "Whenua, lead the way. Take us to the Le-Metru hatch closest to the Coliseum."

"I still say this is a mistake," said Onewa. "We could be walking right into an ambush."

"My visions would have warned me," the Toa of Fire said calmly. "And they haven't. You'll see, Onewa, before you know it we will be safely back on the island with our friends. We are Toa, after all — a few spiders aren't going to stop us."

. . .

An aged pair of eyes watched the Toa depart. The heroes never saw the being who watched them, for he did not wish to be seen. There would be time enough for a meeting later.

He darted through the darkness as if it were bright sunlight, surefooted and swift. Pouks would see to the ash bear's safety, while Iruini led the Suukorak on a futile chase deep into the Archives. He knew the winding, twisted halls better than any being alive. The Visorak would have no hope of catching him.

Norik's task was to keep watch on the Toa Metru. They were walking into danger, and worse, doing it with their eyes wide open. He could not fathom the depths of their recklessness. Did they not have eyes? Could they not see what had taken hold of their city?

Norik's mind flashed back to times past. How many lands had he seen fall to the Visorak? How many thousands of living beings had been brought low by their insatiable hunger for con-quest? And all the while, the faces of Sidorak and

Roodaka loomed over all, laughing as lives were ruined and great works ground into dust.

He picked up the pace. The Toa Metru were moving very quickly, as if in a hurry to meet their doom. And if Norik did not catch them in time, their lives and all hope for this city would be lost forever.

Whenua opened the hatch, slowly and carefully. He looked from side to side, but saw nothing out of the ordinary. *Just your usual quake-ravaged, blacked out city of legends,* he said to himself.

"It's as safe as it's going to be," he whispered. "Come on."

The Toa Metru climbed out of the Archives and onto the street. The Coliseum loomed over them. None of the heroes could look on that imposing edifice and not remember the horrible sight of Matoran being loaded into stasis spheres while Makuta stole the power of an entire city. The earthquake had followed hard upon that moment, but far more than the city was shattered. Something in the Toa Metru had crumbled as well.

"What is our plan?" asked Nuju.

"Get to the Coliseum, down any Vahki guards there, and get the spheres," answered Vakama. "Then we get them out of the city before the Visorak find us."

"How?"

"We could lash together Vahki transports and sail back the way we came. Then we can carry the spheres overland through the Karzahni's lair and back to the island."

"Where do I begin to list the reasons that won't work?" said Nuju.

"Forget it," Vakama replied. "We will worry about getting them to the island once they are safely in our hands. Follow me."

As they moved out behind the Toa of Fire, Matau was struck by the utter silence. He had never heard Le-Metru so quiet. It wasn't just the absence of Matoran voices, though that was eerie in itself. There was no birdsong. Ordinarily, nests of Rahi flyers could be found in the tangle of cables, but now they were all gone. He wanted to think they had simply fled after the earthquake to a more hospitable home, but the Toa of Air knew better. The Visorak had been here, and nothing had been left behind.

Up ahead, Vakama was marching confidently as if he owned the metru. He had not bothered to send a scout ahead or even have Matau keep watch from the air. Onewa and Nuju were so tired of protesting that they were now just going along with whatever the Toa of Fire said.

Next to him, Nokama was lost in her own thoughts. She felt she knew Vakama as well or better than any of the Toa, but his actions now mystified her. He had been so dedicated to living up to Lhikan's memory, yet he was ignoring every lesson the Toa had taught. Where Lhikan was cautious, Vakama had become reckless; where Lhikan valued the wisdom of others, Vakama was ignoring the other Toa to pursue his own course.

Now it felt as if events were rushing to a conclusion, as water rushed over the protodermis falls. Every part of her being screamed they should stop, turn back, run away. Something was closing in on them, something ancient and evil beyond measure. It would seize them, twist them, and taint them with its touch. But when she opened her mouth to speak, the words would not come. Vakama would not turn back on the strength of her bad feeling. He would lead them into a fire pit if it meant fulfilling his promise to Lhikan.

"Almost there," said the Toa of Fire. "When we get there, Whenua, you and Onewa can begin digging passages into the storage chamber. The more openings we have, the faster we can get the job done. The rest of us will try to awaken some of the Matoran so they can help us move the spheres."

"I will high-fly and keep watch while you work," said Matau. "That way, no crawlers can sneak up on us."

"We need every pair of hands below," Vakama replied. "The faster we move, the less chance of any problems."

"I will high-fly and keep watch," Matau repeated. "I don't want to back-walk into a Visorak, thank you, and neither should you."

Vakama shrugged. There was no point in arguing. When they got there, Matau would see they had nothing to worry about and agree to work like the others.

The Keelerak watched the Toa Metru pass below. As Roodaka had predicted, they were on their way to the tall structure that now served as the spawning grounds. Given the opportunity, they would damage the cocoons and delay the fall of Metru Nui.

The spider creatures began to scuttle across their webs. It was their job to make sure the Toa Metru did not get the opportunity to oppose the will of the horde.

They moved as silently as a shadow stealing across the wall. Each member of this squad was a veteran, instincts and skills honed in a thousand marches. Each had savored the fruits of victory countless times, gloating over the sight of foes trapped forever in the center of their webs. It would be no different with these Toa. If anything, the Keelerak found themselves wishing for a greater challenge.

"Why?" Nuju said to himself, loud enough for Onewa to hear.

"Why what, librarian?"

"Why did the Visorak allow us to escape through the Archives? If Whenua is right, and they chose to withdraw, they could have summoned others to strike at us. Yet they let us depart and make our way to our goal."

"Like I said . . . not too bright," said Onewa.

"I wish I had your confidence, brother," said Nuju. "But I cannot help but feel that there are more webs than the ones above us and around us. I think we are walking on one even now, and just when we think we have escaped, it will snap shut around us."

"Amazing," said Onewa. "I have finally found it."

"What?"

"Someone who makes Whenua sound cheerful."

"Quiet!" whispered Vakama. "Watch for Vahki. Maybe we will be lucky and there won't be any around. But you see? All the way to the Coliseum, and not a Visorak in sight."

A swirling, rotating wheel of energy flew from the shadows to strike the Toa of Fire squarely in the back. Instantly, Vakama stopped dead in his tracks, paralyzed by the spinner's force. Before the other Toa could react, they too were struck and all movement frozen — forward movement anyway. Off-balance when he was struck, Whenua toppled over and struck his friends, causing them all to fall hard to the ground.

"Is everyone okay?" asked Vakama.

"Paralyzed," replied Nuju. "But otherwise unharmed."

"We're right behind you, Vakama," said Matau, making no effort to hide his sarcasm. "Literally."

"Bickering won't get us out of this, Matau," admonished Nokama.

"No, but think-talking before charging straight into a trap might have."

"If you have something to say, say it," snapped Vakama.

"Forget it," grumbled Matau.

Any further argument was cut off by the sound of multiple figures approaching. The Toa could do nothing but wait and watch for the intruders. Soon, the Toa were surrounded.

The Visorak bristled with power. Vicious, spider like monstrosities, their mandibles gnashed and slimy webbing oozed from their mouths. Mounted on their backs were what looked like launchers. As the Toa watched, an energy spinner formed inside the launcher of one of the green Visorak and then was fired high into the air. A swarm of bat creatures scattered at its approach. But the spinner was not meant as an attack. It was rather a signal that the battle had been won.

"Vakama, what do we do?" whispered Nokama.

"I . . . I don't know," answered the Toa of Fire, in a voice so low she could barely hear it.

Then the Visorak began to spin their webs . . .

Roodaka smiled as she watched a small group of Visorak crafting another web. This one connected the Coliseum to another of the Knowledge Towers of Ko-Metru. It seemed appropriate that these creatures comprised her army, for in many ways she too created snares for the unwary.

There was far more to web-spinning than simply the right location and a few strands of silk. It had to be reinforced and supported so that if wind or a storm tore a section loose, the entire structure would not collapse. In much the same way, Roodaka's plans were constructed so that no one setback could destroy them. Even events that might seem disastrous at first could be turned to her advantage.

So it had been when word came that the Toa had been captured. The Visorak Keelerak horde that had brought down the Toa Metru owed its loyalty to Sidorak, their king, rather than to her. At heart a conqueror, Sidorak saw in the six Toa only enemies to be destroyed. He had ordered the heroes webbed into cocoons and hoisted high in the air outside the Coliseum, planning to simply have them dashed to their deaths on the ground far below.

It was then that Roodaka took a hand. "Is it to be so simple, Sidorak?" she had asked. "A leader is judged by the quality of his enemies. The Toa are powerful adversaries indeed, and their deaths should be . . . memorable."

Sidorak smiled. Where he ruled through might and intimidation, Roodaka embodied the more subtle qualities that fueled conquest. She understood fear, dread, and the power of symbols to evoke both. Her advice was always welcomed by him, not the least because he hoped she would one day be far more than just an aide in his campaigns.

Most of all, Sidorak trusted Roodaka. That was his first mistake.

"I suppose I could make their deaths more . . . worthy of legend," he agreed.

With her subtle prodding, Sidorak agreed to leave the Toa in the cocoons long enough for them to experience the unique properties of Visorak venom. They would perish just the same, but she would have gained valuable knowledge of the effects of the poison on Toa.

She stepped to the window and looked up to see the Toa in their cocoons, hanging from a Visorak web. Her eyes devoured the sight of them struggling helplessly to free themselves. There was nothing quite so pleasant, she decided, as weak, pitiful creatures striving to avoid their inevitable doom.

9

The six Toa Metru hung in cocoons high above the city streets. All around them, on the rooftops of Metru Nui, hordes of Visorak spiders were assembled to watch their demise. The cocoons were connected to the webs above by only a few thin strands. In time, the weight of the Toa would tear them loose and then it would be a long fall. If they were lucky, their sheer velocity on the way down would be enough to end their lives long before they struck the ground.

"Well, fire-spitter, we can't say you didn't show us the city," Matau muttered. "'Course, we can say that you got us captured, poisoned . . . and seeing as I don't think we've been brought up here for the view, imminently mash-dashed!"

Vakama struggled to think of what to say in reply. His head and body hurt all over. He could feel the barbs of the cocoon biting into him and the Visorak venom coursing through his form. He glanced at the other Toa, now all facing destruction because he had made the wrong decisions.

"I tried to lead you as best I could," he said. "I wish I had been better at it. But if I've learned one thing from all we have been through, it is that I am what I am. And no matter how much I might want to, I can't just change."

A spasm gripped Vakama, sending violent shudders down his body. Suddenly, an arm tore its way free of his cocoon. He looked at it, confused. Surely, that twisted, bizarre limb did not belong to him.

The effect was spreading to the other Toa. Their bodies warped and mutated, masks changing shape, muscles expanding, their very minds feeling like they were being torn apart and reassembled. It was a pain beyond pain, made worse by the certain knowledge that there was no way to stop whatever was happening to them.

"I'm not liking this!" shouted Matau.

Nuju managed to shift his focus from the rapid changes happening to his body. As the Toa's bodies mutated, they were tearing through the webs that made up their cocoons, the only things that were keeping them in the air. At this rate, they would not have to worry about their new forms for very long.

"You're going to like it even less in a moment," he said.

Vakama's mutation had begun first, so his cocoon was the most badly damaged. As Nuju watched, the Toa of Fire tore free of the webbing and plunged into space. One by one the others followed, their strange, animalistic new forms flailing in the air as they fell. Then the Toa of Ice lost his grip as well and plummeted toward the ground.

The ground rushed to greet him. The wind made it impossible to breathe. He shut his eyes, bracing himself for his last moments.

Impact!

But not the kind he was expecting. Someone had slammed into him, cutting off his fall. Now he was being carried away by his rescuer, moving by leaps and bounds across the rubble of the city.

Nuju opened his eyes. The being that held him was like none he had ever seen before. Bent and twisted, it looked like a cross between a Turaga, a Rahkshi, and some other Rahi species. Despite its small stature, it seemed to have no difficulty scaling walls or swinging from loose cables. If Nuju's weight was a burden to the strange creature, it gave no sign.

Their journey came to an end in the ruins of Ga-Metru. The other Toa were already there, all of them transformed into freakish combinations of their own forms and the bodies of beasts. They were confused and horrified by what they had become. Even Matau could not look at his reflection in a puddle of water.

The Toa of Ice turned to ask his savior a question, only to find that all six of the little creatures were gone. *Mysteries built atop other mysteries,* he thought. *And none of them helping to solve the greatest of them all — what have we become?*

His mood was not improved by the discovery that his mask powers no longer worked.

Whether that was a result of damage to the mask itself as a result of the mutation, or some side effect of the transformation on his own mind, he did not know. Even worse, his ice powers no longer responded to his commands. His Toa tools were gone as well, replaced by strange pieces of equipment whose function he could not comprehend.

He looked at his friends — where once they had been powerful, noble Toa, now they resembled something that would be hidden in a sub-level of the Archives. Matau looked by far the worse. Nokama instinctively moved to comfort him.

"It's all right," she whispered.

"All right? You call *this* all right?"

"We're all here. We'll find a way. Together."

"That's what friends do," added Whenua.

Matau got to his feet with surprising quickness and advanced on Vakama. "I don't hear you saying that, smelt-head. What's the matter — too busy think-planning another master plan? Maybe you can get us killed next time, instead of just turned into monster-beasts!"

Vakama stepped away, snarling, "I'm through making plans."

"Well, that's the first happy-cheer thing I've heard since I turned ugly!"

Nuju frowned. Bickering was going to get them nowhere. Their future as Toa, or whatever they might be now, was going to depend on the decisions made in the next few moments.

"Regardless of how we look, it might be better if we use our energy to find out why we have become . . . whatever it is we are," he said.

"The sooner we do that, the sooner we can rescue the Matoran," Nokama agreed. "But where do we start?"

Matau shrugged. "How are we to be-saving when we are the ones need-saving?"

"If you are wise, if you wish to be what you once were, you will listen."

All six Toa turned at the strange voice, half wise sage, half snarling beast. The strange beings that had saved them from their fall had reappeared, seemingly out of thin air. They regarded the Toa, not with fear or horror, but with sadness and resolve.

Norik spoke again, "You have become something both more and less than what you were," he said. "You walk a road that is all too familiar . . . we know how it begins, and we know how it can end. You must act now, Toa, or there is no hope for you or your city."

A surge of hope ran through the Toa. True, these creatures resembled old foes a little too much for comfort, but if they knew how this change could be reversed . . .

"Tell us how to undo this, wise ones, and I'll personally build a field full of statues in your honor," growled Onewa.

"You would be doing Metru Nui and the Matoran, as well as us, a great service," said Nokama.

"We know of your plight," Norik replied. "We have been living in the shadows of this city since before the cataclysm. We are aware of what happened to the Matoran, as well as what terrible plans the Visorak have for them. But we can do little to stop them. It is you who must act."

"How?" demanded Nuju. For some reason, the riddles these beings were speaking sparked anger in him. It felt strange, for he was never one to let his emotions get the best of him. Yet at the same time, rage seemed like the most natural reaction to this situation. It was something he would have to think long and hard about.

"Keetongu," said Norik.

Nuju glanced at his fellow Toa. It was obvious that none of them understood the term.

"Keetongu is a powerful creature gifted in knowledge of venoms and their counteragents," Norik said. "And he is our only hope of standing against the Visorak horde. If you are to be the Toa you once were, it is Keetongu you must seek."

"But what are we now?" asked Nokama. She too was having a hard time keeping her temper in check.

"The Visorak cocoons injected you with Hordika venom. It now courses within you. If it is not neutralized, it will take root, and Hordika you will be forever. Half-Toa, half-beast, prisoners of your own instincts, your own rage . . . until the day your Rahi nature takes hold completely, and you are no better than gibbering things bringing destruction wherever you roam."

Nokama shuddered at the thought. This could not be their destiny! It could not have been why Mata Nui blessed them with the power of Toa!

"I am a Rahaga," the being continued. "Norik is my name. These others are Gaaki, Bomonga, Kualus, Pouks, and Iruini."

None of the Toa knew quite what to say. It was hard enough to believe all this had happened to them, let alone that such bizarre looking creatures were their only hope. Finally, Nokama spoke up. "Rahaga, can you take us to this Keetongu?"

The Rahaga called Iruini laughed. Norik shot him a stern look, then turned back to Nokama. "What Iruini so inappropriately suggests is that this will be . . . difficult. We Rahaga came to Metru Nui in search of Keetongu, and there are those of us that, well, doubt his existence entirely."

"Oh, wonderful," said Onewa. "Our only hope is a myth."

"And you?" Nuju asked Norik. "What do you believe?"

"I believe in legends," said Norik.

"Then so must we," agreed Nokama.

"Wait," interjected Matau. "Shouldn't we group-talk about this? What do you say, Onewa? Whenua? Mask-melter?"

The Toa of Stone and the Toa of Earth said nothing. They had both dared to hope that their transformation might be reversed, only to find out that the whole thing hung on nothing more than simply another legend. Vakama never took his eyes from the ground as he said, "I say we returned to Metru Nui to rescue Matoran, not to hunt down mythical beasts."

"And you have a way of doing this?" Norik asked sharply. "Perhaps using your new Hordika powers? Powers you have not yet learned to use."

"I don't know," said the Toa of Fire. Something in his voice told Nokama he was dangerously close to an explosion.

"Don't know, or don't want to include the rest of us in your plans?" Norik prodded.

"Either," Vakama replied. Then he rose and stalked away.

"Vakama!" Nokama cried after him.

"I will talk with him," said Norik.

"What about us?" asked Matau.

Norik gave him a smile, one laced with a hint of menace. "Prepare yourselves. We've a legend to prove."

It was some time before Vakama returned to the group. An uneasy silence lingered for a long while before he spoke.

"I can't tell you all what to do," the Toa of Fire said. "It's obvious that my orders led us to this disaster. It's equally obvious that some of you no longer wish my company," he said, looking at Matau and Onewa.

"Vakama, they didn't —" Nokama began.

Vakama cut her off. "But I think we can all agree that our problems pale next to those of the Matoran. We have to be sure they are safe before we can worry about how to reverse this transformation."

Nuju nodded. "As much as I wish it were otherwise, you are right. Placing the Matoran first puts us at risk of being Hordika forever, something I would not wish on anyone. But seeing to ourselves before saving them may doom an entire population to this fate, or worse."

"We are Toa-heroes, even if we don't look like it," said Matau. "We have two problems — rescuing the Matoran from the Coliseum, and then getting them out of this city. If you will think-plan on the first, I may have an idea of how to do the second."

"Then let's get started," Onewa said, bounding on top of a pile of rubble. "We are not getting any younger, and Matau is not getting any better looking."

. . .

Norik watched the Toa talk and plan as they journeyed back to Le-Metru. It was good that they had a mission and goal in mind to keep them from thinking about their fate. He knew better than most what Toa were capable of, but in his heart, he doubted that these heroes could avoid their doom.

He signaled to the other Rahaga to spread out and keep to the shadows. If there were Visorak near, the Rahaga would spot them. The Rahaga had survived this long by avoiding the hordes, running, hiding . . . but no more.

Metru Nui will be our final showdown with these creatures from the pit, he told himself. *And before it is done, either Visorak or Rahaga will be no more.*

Roodaka sat on the throne that had once belonged to Makuta. Sidorak had departed to gather his legions in preparation for hunting the Toa Hordika. He would rely, as he always did, on the overwhelming force of numbers to achieve his ends. The Visorak would sweep through the city like a plague, never resting until their prey had been run to earth.

But will that be enough? she wondered. *These are Toa . . . mutated, yes, burdened with the dual nature of the Hordika, but Toa just the same. This is their city. They know its hiding places, and they have the cursed Rahaga to aid them. With luck and skill, they might evade the hordes.*

That would never do. She needed the Toa to achieve her ultimate plan, and by Makuta's dark power, she would have them.

The queen of the Visorak rose and walked to the massive sundial that dominated the chamber. Once this device had measured the amount of time remaining before Metru Nui was wracked by cataclysm. Now it counted down the hours the Toa Hordika had left to live.

Roodaka smiled. Let Sidorak lead his legions on a chase through streets and alleyways. She would make plans of her own, plans so subtle and so devious that even the master of shadows would applaud, were he free.

Soon, she thought. *Very soon, now hand will the light be banished from this city, and darkness left to rule forevermore.*

And deep in the bowels of the Coliseum, the sleeping Matoran trembled in the grip of nightmares that would not end . . .

EPILOGUE

Turaga Vakama took a deep breath and let it out slowly. He had thought that somehow sharing this tale after so many years would relieve some of his burden. But it had not. If anything, it made the wounds of so many years ago feel freshly made. *Perhaps Nuju was right,* he thought. *Perhaps no good can come of this.*

Tahu Nuva was silent for a very long time. Vakama expected horror or revulsion, but the Toa's mask did not betray his feelings. Finally, the red-hued hero leaned forward and clasped the Turaga's hand.

"You survived much to come to these shores," said Tahu. "More than any of us ever knew. And there is more to your tale, is there not?"

"Yes, Tahu."

"Will I have to beg to hear it?"

"No. Despite what my brothers may wish, the time of secrets and lies is over with. You made a choice to hear the tale of the Toa Hordika, and so you shall. As you have seen, sometimes we can be as foolish as any sand snipe and as blind as an ice bat."

"Meaning what, Turaga?"

Vakama rose, using his staff to support himself. "Meaning you are Toa, not children who need to be protected from the truth. We knew all that went on in those years, and Makuta knew, but you did not. That ignorance might have cost you your lives. Hiding all this from you was as great an error as any we committed as Toa Metru."

Tahu raised his sword and shot a bolt of flame high into the sky. "The other Toa must hear this tale, Vakama. It is a one of triumph, after all."

The Turaga shook his head, confused. Triumph? Had Tahu not been listening at all? "I do not understand you, Toa Tahu."

"Well, you overcame, didn't you? You saved

the Matoran, you became Turaga . . . you were victorious."

Turaga Vakama laughed. It was a sad and hollow sound. "Victorious, were we? Perhaps, in your eyes, that might be so. But we paid a price for that victory, Tahu, and so did every Matoran . . . Makuta's bones, what a price we paid."

No more words would be spoken until the other Toa Nuva arrived. When they were all assembled, Vakama resumed his tale . . .